FEB   2014   CB

D1505717

T1-BLO-545

VICTORIA JUSTICE

By Abigail Shea

 Gareth Stevens
Publishing

Please visit our website, www.garethstevens.com. For a free color catalog of all our high-quality books, call toll free 1-800-542-2595 or fax 1-877-542-2596.

Library of Congress Cataloging-in-Publication Data

Shea, Abigail.
Victoria Justice / by Abigail Shea.
  p. cm. — (Rising stars)
Includes index.
ISBN 978-1-4339-8990-2 (pbk.)
ISBN 978-1-4339-8991-9 (6-pack)
ISBN 978-1-4339-8989-6 (library binding)
1. Justice, Victoria, — 1993- — Juvenile literature. 2. Actors — United States — Biography — Juvenile literature. 3. Singers — United States — Biography — Juvenile literature. I. Title.
PN2287.J87 S54 2014
921—d23

First Edition

Published in 2014 by Gareth Stevens Publishing
111 East 14th Street, Suite 349
New York, NY 10003

Copyright © 2014 Gareth Stevens Publishing

Designer: Nick Domiano
Editor: Therese Shea

Photo credits: Cover, pp. 1, 13 Steve Granitz/WireImage/Getty Images; p. 5 Don Arnold/ WireImage/Getty Images; p. 7 SGranitz/WireImage/Getty Images; p. 9 Alberto E. Rodriguez/ Getty Images Entertainment/Getty Images; p. 11 Mark Von Holden/WireImage/Getty Images; pp. 15, 17 Charley Gallay/WireImage/Getty Images; p. 19 Imeh Akpanudosen/ Getty Images Sport/Getty Images; p. 21 Joe Kohen/Wire Image/Getty Images; p. 23 Larry Busacca/Getty Images Entertainment/Getty Images; p. 25 Frazer Harrison/Getty Images Entertainment/Getty Images; pp. 27, 29 Christopher Polk/Getty Images Entertainment/ Getty Images.

Contents

Hollywood Star

Victoria Justice was born in Hollywood, Florida. She was meant to be a star in Hollywood, California!

5

Young Victoria

Victoria was born on February 19, 1993. Her full name is Victoria Dawn Justice. When Victoria was 8, she decided she wanted to act.

7

Victoria and her family moved to California in 2003. Victoria went to a special school for acting.

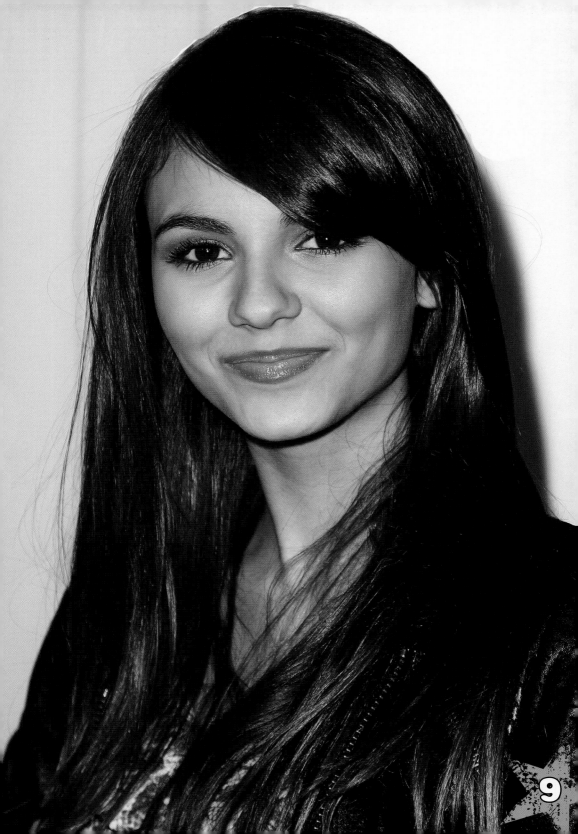

9

Big Break

At first, Victoria appeared in commercials. Then, she had small roles on the TV shows *Gilmore Girls* and *The Suite Life of Zack & Cody*.

11

In 2005, Victoria got a role in the TV show *Zoey 101*. She played a girl named Lola. Victoria was on the show until 2008.

Time to Shine

In 2009, Victoria was in a TV musical called *Spectacular!* She sang three songs. Victoria appeared on the show *iCarly*, too.

15

In 2010, Victoria began to star in her own TV show, *Victorious*. She records many songs for the show. She plays Tori, a student at a Hollywood high school.

Victorious made Victoria discover her love for singing and dancing. She had taken many classes when she was young. Finally, they came in handy!

In 2010, Victoria sang in the Thanksgiving Day Parade in New York City. She has gone on tour, too.

21

In 2011, an album of *Victorious* songs came out. It was at the top of the charts. The biggest hit was the song "Freak the Freak Out."

23

Movies and More

In 2012, Victoria appeared in a movie called *Fun Size*. She played a girl who loses her little brother when they go trick-or-treating on Halloween.

25

Victorious won two Kids' Choice Awards in 2012. Victoria plans to keep starring in the show.

Dream Big

Victoria said, "Never let anyone take away your dream." She didn't. Now she's a star!

29

Timeline

1993 Victoria Justice is born on February 19.

2003 Victoria and her family move to California.

2005 Victoria gets a role on the TV show *Zoey 101*.

2009 Victoria is in *Spectacular!*

2010 Victoria stars in *Victorious*.

2010 Victoria sings in the Thanksgiving Day Parade.

2011 The *Victorious* album comes out.

2012 Victoria stars in *Fun Size*.

2012 *Victorious* wins two Kids' Choice Awards.

30

For More Information

Books

Leavitt, Amie Jane. *Victoria Justice*. Hockessin, DE: Mitchell Lane Publishing, 2011.

Tieck, Sarah. *Victoria Justice: Famous Actress & Singer*. Minneapolis, MN: ABDO Publishing, 2013.

Websites

About Victoria Justice
www.nick.com/celebrity/victoria-justice/
Find videos of Victoria performing.

Victoria Justice
www.imdb.com/name/nm1842439/
See what movies and shows Victoria has coming out.

Victoria Justice's Official Website
www.victoriajustice.net
Read the latest news on Victoria.

Publisher's note to educators and parents: Our editors have carefully reviewed these websites to ensure that they are suitable for students. Many websites change frequently, however, and we cannot guarantee that a site's future contents will continue to meet our high standards of quality and educational value. Be advised that students should be closely supervised whenever they access the Internet.

Glossary

award: a prize given for doing something well

commercial: a break during a TV or radio show that tries to sell something

musical: a play or show that uses singing, music, and dancing to tell a story

record: to make a copy of music that can be played again and again

tour: a trip to many places in order to play and sing music for people

Index

32